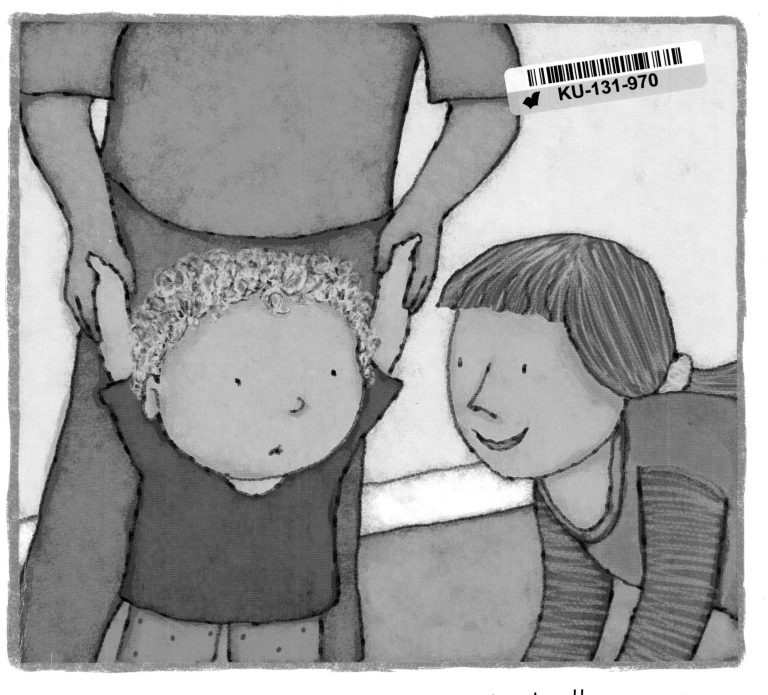

Hello! Remember me? What shall we play?

You can choose a toy. This is my best one.

Baby Sitter

ILLUSTRATED BY JESS STOCKHAM

Child's Play (International) Ltd
Swindon   Auburn ME   Sydney
© 2009 Ch   Aberdeenshire   Printed in China

Come in! I'm nearly ready to go out.

See you later! What will we do now?

Mother Duck said "Quack, Quack, Quack!"

Look at my animals. I can dance and sing!

We can use these. What will I *build*?

I've made a car. Look how fast it goes!

I'm good at drawing! I like green best.

It's your turn! Where does this card go?

I'd like some vegetables. Any carrots?

What's in your basket? Card, please!

I'm hungry now! What shall we drink?

This tastes sweet. Do you like crackers?

Let's clear up all the toys. This is heavy!

Up the stairs, 1..2..3! Bang bang, toot toot!

What's the rabbit saying? It's like my rabbit!

My wings are flapping. I've made a bird.

My arm's stuck! I'll help you.

Look at me! I can do it all by myself.

My teeth are so clean! Where's my cup?

Sleepy now! Teddy, too. One more story!

Night night, little one. Sleep tight!